MARC BROWN

ARTHUR LOST in the MUSEUM

A Sticker Book

P9-DMC-649

Random House 🏠 New York

www.stepintoreading.com

Educators and librarians, for a variety of teaching tools, visit us at www.randomhouse.com/teachers

Library of Congress Cataloging-in-Publication Data
Brown, Marc Tolon.
Arthur lost in the museum / Marc Brown.
p. cm. — (Step into reading. Step 3) "A Sticker Book."
SUMMARY: Arthur goes with his class on a field trip to the museum,
but takes a wrong turn when heading for the bathroom.
ISBN 0-375-82973-3 (trade) — ISBN 0-375-92973-8 (lib. bdg.)
[1. School field trips—Fiction. 2. Museums—Fiction. 3. Aardvark—Fiction.]
I. Title. II. Series: Step into reading. Step 3 book.
PZ7.B81618Anaj 2005 [E]—dc22 2004027623

Printed in the United States of America First Edition 10 9 8 7

The bus stopped at the museum.
Arthur's class got off.
Arthur started to run
up the steps.

"Stop!" shouted Mr. Ratburn.
"You must all stay with me.
I don't want anyone
getting lost."

3

"Today we will visit
the Hall of America,"
said Mr. Ratburn.
Arthur raised his hand.
"Save your question, Arthur,
until we get there,"
said his teacher.
"Now follow me, boys and girls."

Serogia

They walked by
the Hall of Dinosaurs.
Arthur raised his hand again.
"No, Arthur, we do not have time
for the dinosaurs today,"
said Mr. Ratburn.
"That's not what I wanted to ask,"
mumbled Arthur.
But his teacher just kept walking.

"Here we are," said Mr. Ratburn.
"The rooms in here
tell the story of our country.
You'll see how Indians lived
before the Pilgrims came,"
he said.
Arthur raised his hand again.
"Okay, Arthur," said Mr. Ratburn.
"What is your question?"
"May I go to the bathroom?"
Arthur asked.
Everyone laughed.

"Yes, Arthur," said Mr. Ratburn.
"The boys' room is around
the corner.
It's the first door on your left."

Arthur ran down the hall.

He turned the corner

and went into the first door—

on the right.

"It sure is dark in here,"
said Arthur to himself.
He saw another door.
"Maybe the toilets are in here,"
he said.

He opened the door
and stepped into a room
filled with Indians
sitting by a tepee.
"Help!" he screamed.

Then he saw that the Indians
were not alive.
They were models.
One wall was glass.
And there was Mr. Ratburn
telling his class about the Indians.
But no one was listening to him.
They were all laughing
and pointing at Arthur
with the Indians.

"I'm in big trouble," said Arthur,
"if I don't get out of here fast."
He ran out the door
and left the Indians behind him.

Here are some stickers to use in *Arthur Lost in the Museum*. Each of these stickers matches one of the blue words in the story. Find each blue word and put the matching sticker on it.

My Own Arthur Story

by ....

Can you write and illustrate
a story about Arthur's dream of
the dinosaur days? Here are some
stickers to get you started. Have fun!

"What's so funny?"
asked Mr. Ratburn.
He turned around and
saw only Indians making baskets
and arrows.

Arthur crept along the dark hall
to the next door.
"I sure hope
   this is the boys' bathroom,"
   he sighed.

But it wasn't a bathroom.

It was a room showing

the Pilgrims' first Thanksgiving.

And Arthur's teacher was telling
his class all about it.
Everyone laughed
when they saw Arthur.
Mr. Ratburn turned to see
what they were laughing at.
But not before Arthur
became a Pilgrim boy.

When Mr. Ratburn's class left,
Arthur took off the Pilgrim hat.
"I've got to go NOW!" he said.
He left in a hurry.

He ran down the dark hall . . .

and he found the boys' room—

just in time!

Arthur found his class
by a room with
George Washington.
"What took you so long, Arthur?"
asked Mr. Ratburn.
"I was making history,"
said Arthur.